Disney's Aladdin

Story adapted by Ann Braybrooks
Illustrated by Phil Ortiz and Serge Michaels

A GOLDEN BOOK • NEW YORK
Western Publishing Company, Inc., Racine, Wisconsin 53404

One night long ago two horsemen raced across the Arabian desert, chasing an enchanted, winged medallion. When it stopped, the men watched in awe as the sand rose up to form the entrance to a cave. It was shaped like a huge tiger's head with an open mouth.

"At last—the Cave of Wonders!" marveled Jafar, the Sultan's chief adviser. He turned to his companion, Gazeem. "Remember, bring me the lamp first. Then the rest of the treasure is yours."

As Gazeem stepped into the cave, the voice of the tiger-god boomed, "Only one who is worthy may enter here!"

With a roar, the cave's entrance clamped shut, trapping Gazeem inside. The tiger's head quickly dissolved into the sand.

"We must get that lamp!" Jafar said to Iago, his wicked parrot. "Obviously Gazeem was not worthy enough to enter the cave. We must find the person who is."

The next day, in the nearby city of Agrabah, a poor young peasant named Aladdin and his pet monkey, Abu, were being chased through the marketplace for taking a loaf of bread. Aladdin and Abu wove in and out of the market stalls, until they managed to get away from the palace guards and drop to safety behind a high wall.

Aladdin and Abu could hardly wait to eat. But when Aladdin saw two hungry children staring up at him, he gave them the bread.

That night Aladdin and Abu returned to their rooftop home. "I know you're hungry, too," Aladdin said to Abu. "But things will change. Someday we'll be rich and live like kings!"

Meanwhile, at the Sultan's palace, Princess Jasmine was not at all happy. According to the law, she must marry a prince by her next birthday, which was only three days away.

"Father, I don't like being forced into marriage," Jasmine confessed. "All the men I have met were either selfish or conceited. When I marry, I want it to be for love and not because of the law."

"It's not only the law, Jasmine," replied the Sultan. "I want to make sure that someone will care for you when I'm gone."

But the Sultan's words did not make Jasmine feel any better. In fact, she was so sad that she decided to run away, even though she had never been outside the palace grounds. Soon she found herself in the marketplace—and in trouble.

Without thinking, Jasmine had taken an apple from a cart.

"You'd better pay for that!" said the fruit seller.

"But I can't pay," cried Jasmine. "I have no money!"

Suddenly Aladdin dashed up and claimed to be her brother. "She didn't mean any harm," he told the fruit seller. "She's a little crazy."

Just then Abu grabbed some apples, and the fruit seller called the palace guards.

Aladdin and Jasmine went racing through the marketplace.

"We'll soon be safe," said Aladdin. But he was so dazzled by her beauty that he did not see a guard following them.

Suddenly the guard seized Aladdin. "Unhand him!" Jasmine cried.

"Princess Jasmine!" said the guard, surprised. "Jafar has ordered us to arrest this peasant and take him to the dungeon."

"We'll see about that," said Jasmine. She hurried back to the palace to find Jafar.

Jasmine found Jafar in his chambers. "Why do you
[w]ant that young man from the marketplace?" she
[d]emanded.

"He was a criminal," answered Jafar, "and he has
[al]ready paid for his crimes with his life."

"Oh, how could you?" cried Jasmine, heartbroken.

Jasmine did not know that Jafar was lying. By using
[m]agic, the evil adviser had discovered that Aladdin was
[th]e worthy one who could enter the Cave of Wonders.

Late that night Jafar disguised himself as a crippled old prisoner
and visited Aladdin in the dungeon.

"I can set you free and reward you well," whispered the sly
Jafar, "if you will help me find a special lamp."

Although Aladdin was suspicious, he said, "It's a deal."

They slipped out of the dungeon and hurried off to the desert.
Soon they stood before the tiger-god and heard its booming voice.
"Proceed. Touch nothing but the lamp."

Aladdin stepped inside the cave.

Aladdin and Abu found themselves in a huge cavern filled with coins and jewels. "Look at all this treasure!" Aladdin exclaimed. "Just a handful would make me rich."

Suddenly a beautifully woven carpet came to life and began floating around them. "Look!" cried Aladdin. "There's even a magic carpet."

The magic carpet understood that Aladdin was looking for the lamp and quickly led Aladdin and Abu into another chamber.

"There's the lamp!" Aladdin cried, pointing to the top of a high staircase. "Wait here, Abu. And don't touch anything!"

Aladdin climbed the stairs. Just as he reached for the lamp, he looked back and saw Abu grab a large glittering ruby.

"No, Abu!" shouted Aladdin. But it was too late! The Cave of Wonders began to collapse around them.

With the magic carpet to protect them, Aladdin and Abu
survived. But they found themselves trapped inside a dark
cave. "That old man tricked us for a worthless old lamp!" said
Aladdin. As he spoke, he rubbed the lamp. To his astonishment,
the lamp began to glow and, in seconds, an enormous genie
emerged.

The Genie grinned and said, "Wow! Does it feel good to be out of that lamp! Nice to meet you, master!"

"Wait a minute," said Aladdin. "Am I your *master*?"

"That's right, laddie boy," answered the Genie. "I can grant you three wishes. But I can't kill anybody! I can't make anybody fall in love! And I can't bring people back from the dead. But I can get you out of this cave." And the Genie did just that!

After the carpet had flown them to an oasis, Aladdin started thinking. "What would *you* wish for, Genie?" he asked.

"I would wish for my freedom," answered the Genie.

"Then I will set you free with my third wish," promised Aladdin. "But for my first wish, there's a smart, beautiful princess I would like to impress. Can you make me a prince?"

"One prince coming up!" said the Genie as he turned the ragged peasant into an elegant prince.

The next day, while Aladdin was traveling back to the city,
Jafar conferred with his pet parrot, Iago. "I can make the
Sultan do whatever I want by using my magical cobra staff to
hypnotize him," said Jafar. "And as soon as the Sultan agrees
to make Jasmine my bride, I will control the kingdom!"

That afternoon Jafar began to present his marriage plan to the Sultan. But before he could finish, the doors to the throne room burst open and a handsome prince entered.

"I am Prince Ali Ababwa, and I have traveled from afar to seek your daughter's hand in marriage," announced Aladdin, disguised as the prince.

"How dare you!" cried Jasmine, who had slipped in from the garden. "You have no right to decide my future."

Before Aladdin could answer, Jasmine ran from the room.

Aladdin, fearing he had lost Jasmine forever, asked the Genie for advice.

"Why don't you tell Jasmine the truth?" the Genie suggested.

"No way!" said Aladdin. "But I will try to see her."

Aladdin found Jasmine in her room. Before he knew it, she was accepting his invitation to go for a ride on the magic carpet.

During the trip, Jasmine realized that Prince Ali was the young man from the marketplace. "Why did you lie to me?" she asked.

"Oh, sometimes I dress as a commoner," answered Aladdin, still afraid to tell the truth. "But I really am a prince."

Later Aladdin and Jasmine returned to the palace. They
kissed good night and, at that moment, Aladdin knew she cared
for him, too.

"My life is finally starting to go right," Aladdin thought. But
seconds later the palace guards seized him.

On Jafar's orders, the guards bound and gagged Aladdin.
They carried him to a high cliff and tossed him into the sea.

The lamp tumbled from its hiding place in Aladdin's turban.
Just then the Genie appeared. "Don't you want me to save your
life?" he pleaded.

Nodding desperately, Aladdin made his second wish.

The Genie helped Aladdin make his way back to the palace.
He found Jafar in Jasmine's room. Aladdin seized the cobra staff
and broke the hypnotic spell Jafar had cast on the Sultan.

"Your Highness," Aladdin declared, "not only did Jafar order me
to be killed, but he's been hypnotizing you with this staff."

"Guards!" the Sultan commanded. "Arrest Jafar, the traitor!"

But it was too late, for Jafar had escaped. It was not too late,
however, for the Sultan to see that Aladdin and Jasmine had fallen
in love.

Later that day Aladdin was thinking about Jasmine and about his third wish. He summoned the Genie from the lamp. "I'm sorry," Aladdin told him, "but I can't set you free. I may need your help if I marry Jasmine and become the next Sultan."

After the disappointed Genie returned to the lamp, Aladdin thought he heard Jasmine calling and went to look for her. Meanwhile Iago sneaked into Aladdin's room and stole the magic lamp for Jafar, who was lurking in the throne room.

Iago rushed to the throne room with the lamp. Jafar quickly summoned the Genie. "Make me Sultan," Jafar commanded, "and make Jasmine and her father my slaves." Sadly the Genie obeyed.

"Better still," Jafar continued, "for my second wish, make me the most powerful sorcerer in the world!"

Again the Genie obeyed. As the sorcerer, Jafar changed Prince Ali back into the peasant Aladdin and sent him far, far away.

Fortunately, the magic carpet and Abu had been banished with him. Aladdin asked the magic carpet to take them back to Agrabah so that he could free the Genie and destroy Jafar.

When Aladdin appeared in the palace, Jafar could not believe his eyes. "How often do I have to get rid of you?" he roared.

Aladdin knew that he couldn't overcome Jafar's magic, but he could try to trick him. "You are powerful," Aladdin said, "but a genie's magic is more powerful. Why not become a genie?"

Jafar made his third wish. To everyone's astonishment, he began to shrink smaller and smaller. He had forgotten one very important thing—every genie is imprisoned in a lamp!

Now the Sultan and Jasmine were rid of Jafar, and Aladdin happily made his third wish to free the Genie.

"No matter what anyone says, you'll always be a prince to me," the grateful Genie told Aladdin.

"That's right!" exclaimed the Sultan. "From this day forth, the princess is free to marry whomever she wants!"

Of course Jasmine chose Aladdin. The young man's greatest wish had come true!

LAKE COUNTY PUBLIC LIBRARY
INDIANA

AD	FF	MU
AV	GR	NC
BO	HI	SJ
CL	HO	MAY 12 94 CN L
DS	LS	

THIS BOOK IS RENEWABLE BY PHONE OR IN PERSON IF THERE IS NO RESERVE
WAITING OR FINE DUE.

LCP #0390